BLACK and WHITE

by Donna Gillum

illustrated by Don Berry

This Book Belongs To:

____

given by:

____

 ISBN 1-4196-2632-9

Book Dedications

This book is dedicated to my beautiful little princess. May God always smile upon you.

To my family: Thank you for all of your love and kindness.

To my students: Always listen and learn. Thank you for being the sunshine in my life.

To Katie: Thank you for being such an inspiration.

Don Berry: Thank you so much for being the ram in the bush. I can't wait for the next project.

To Grandma: You are my guardian angel.

My sister and I love to hang around the house and watch t.v.
For I am only eight years old and my sister is only three.

Sometimes we play in our backyard with our dog Lucky and our cat Sue
For these two animals are not enough, we'd rather have a zoo.

We'd have so many pets to choose from
And we'd have so much fun.

The hip-po-pa-ta-mus, you see
Would be my favorite one.

My sister likes the zebras
Because they're black and white.

She says that these two colors
Together are out of sight.

My grandmother heard her say this once
And sat us down to tell us a story.

About these two colors, black and white
And she said that it was our History.

My sister said, "Why is it History?"
"Why couldn't it be hers?"

Grandma laughed and said, "Listen child,
Hush, and don't say a word."

Long ago there were people who looked like you and me.
They were in a land called Africa and there they were free.

But one day a group of people came to take them from their land.
They brought them here to America, but this language they did not understand.

They were forced to work very hard and money they did not receive.
This type of treatment was given a name – they called it SLAVERY.

Some of the slaves worked hard in their master's house
While others worked in the fields.
Most were separated from their families.
And they braved this ordeal.

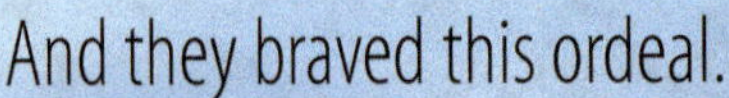

In 1863, Abraham Lincoln passed the Emancipation Proclamation. This law freed all of the slaves in states within our nation.

After that law was passed
It was still hard for us.

Because even in the 1960's
We couldn't ride in the front of the bus.

We were told to go to the back
Because we were considered dark

But one woman helped to changed all of that
Her name was Rosa Parks.

Rosa Parks
1913 ~ 2005

There are many people like you and me
Who fought for our civil rights.

Some did it very peacefully
While others ended up in fights.

You'll hear about such people
Like Malcolm X and Dr. King

Who fought with all of their might
And said, "Let freedom ring."

WE MARCH FOR
INTEGRATED SCHOOLS NOW!
WE DEMAND
DECENT HOUSING NOW!
WE DEMAND
AN END TO BIAS NOW!

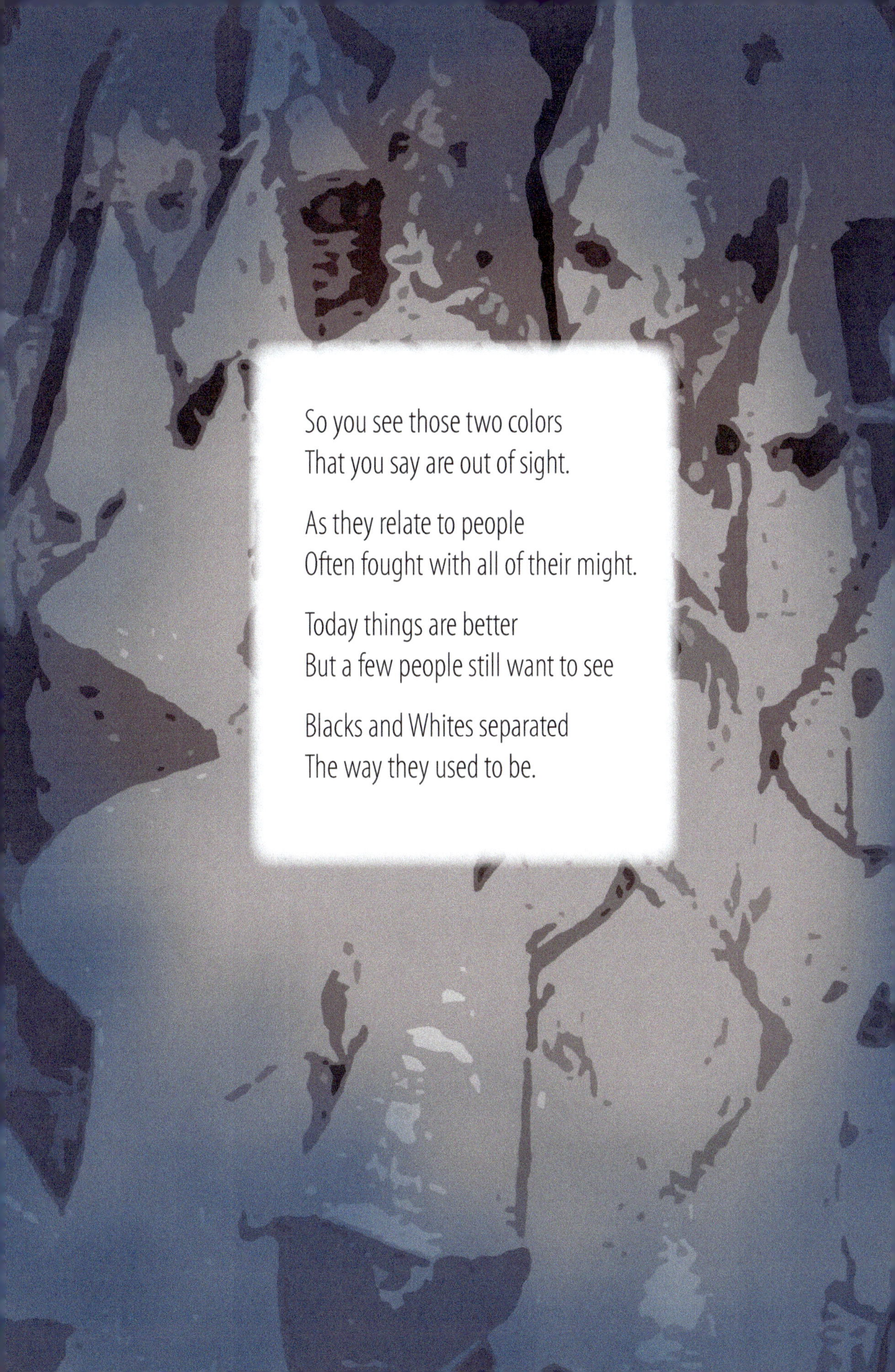

So you see those two colors
That you say are out of sight.

As they relate to people
Often fought with all of their might.

Today things are better
But a few people still want to see

Blacks and Whites separated
The way they used to be.

This story that I've just told you
Is one that you will hear again.

But keep in mind that you shouldn't
Judge someone by the color of their skin.

In God's eyes we are all the same
And child you are right.

Indeed these two colors, Black and White,
Together are out of sight.

The End

www.ingramcontent.com/pod-product-compliance
Lightning Source LLC
LaVergne TN
LVHW080043170826
845677LV00024B/1420

* 9 7 9 8 8 8 8 9 5 6 2 4 3 *